A DAY *in the* LIFE *of* A TUDOR CRIMINAL

Alan Childs
Illustrated by Adam Hook

WAYLAND

A Day in the Life

Titles in the series

A Roman Centurion
A Tudor Criminal
A Victorian Street Seller
A World War II Evacuee

Editor: Jason Hook
Designer: Jan Sterling
Picture Research: Shelley Noronha
Production Controller: Tracy Fewtrell

First published in 1999 by Wayland Publishers Ltd,
61 Western Road, Hove, East Sussex BN3 1JD, England

Find Wayland on the Internet at http://www.wayland.co.uk

British Library Cataloguing in Publication Data
Childs, Alan, 1942–
   1. Criminals – England – History – 16th Century – Juvenile literature 2. Great
   Britain – History – Tudors, 1484–1603 – Juvenile Literature 3. England – Social
   Conditions – 16th century – Juvenile Literature
   I. Title
   942'.05

   ISBN 0 7502 2642 0

Printed and bound in Italy by EuroGrafica.

Cover picture: (foreground) the pickpocket; (background) the Tower of London.

Picture Acknowledgements: The publishers would like to thank the following for
permission to publish their pictures: AKG Photo, London 20 (bottom); © Board of
Trustees of the Armouries *TR 98.259* 4, *TR 98.0257* 8 (top), *TR.822 21* (bottom);
Bridgeman Art Library, London/New York /Private Collection 11 (bottom), 19, 28
(top), 29 (bottom), /Hatfield House, Hertfordshire 7 (top), /Manor House, Stanton
Harcourt, Oxon 9 (top), /Society of Antiquaries, London 11 (top), /Earl of Pembroke,
Wilton House 27 (bottom); Edinburgh University Library 7 (bottom); ET Archive 14,
27 (top); Finc Art Photographic Library, London 8 (bottom); Folger Shakespeare
Library 28 (bottom); Fotomas Index 5 (bottom), 10, 13 (top), 15 (bottom), 18 (top),
23, 24, 26 (left); Hever Castle Ltd 22 (top); John Tramper, Shakespeare's Globe 18
(bottom); Michael Holford 25 (bottom); Museum of London 13 (bottom), 29 (left);
National Portrait Gallery 20 (top); Robert Harding *cover*, 15 (top), 21 (top), 26
(right); Mary Evans 5 (top), 9 (bottom), 12.

**All Wayland books encourage children to read and
help them improve their literacy.**

 The contents page, page numbers, headings and index
help locate specific pieces of information.

The glossary reinforces alphabetic knowledge and
extends vocabulary.

The further information section suggests other books
dealing with the same subject.

Find out more about how this book is specifically
relevant to the National Literacy Strategy on page 30.

CONTENTS

Meet our Tudor criminal. Hal is 12 summers old, and lives rough on the streets of London during the reign of Queen Elizabeth I. He is a likeable rogue, who is well known to the local cutpurses and vagabonds. To survive, he steals crusts and picks pockets – a 'trade' he learnt from his father. Hal has seen the inside of prison more times than he cares to remember. It is no surprise that a day in his life begins in Newgate gaol.

The candle-clock that appears throughout the book is a way of telling the time which was invented over a thousand years ago. It takes an hour for each ring of wax to burn down, as you will see.

THE CRIMINAL

Hal wakes suddenly, and staggers to his feet. Dusty sunlight drifts through the high, barred windows of his cell in Newgate prison. The smell from the lavatory or 'jakes' is unbearable. One poor wretch huddles against the wall. His hands are held by thumbscrews. 'He's going to be hanged today on Tyburn Tree,' another prisoner laughs.

▲ Thumbscrews were used both to torture prisoners and as handcuffs.

In the sixteenth century, convicted criminals were held in gaol only until they could receive other punishments. Thieves and murderers in London's Newgate gaol were soon to be flogged or executed. Other prisoners were awaiting trial. But many gaols held people who simply owed money. If they could not pay off their debts, they might die in prison without ever having committed a crime.

◀ A young pickpocket could find himself in gaol for a long time, if he did not have enough money to pay a fine.

'The beadles and watchmen are in the pay of the keepers of both the Counters [gaols], and for every man they commit they receive a groat, and ... for gain will, upon any light or slight fault, carry any man that comes in their way to prison.' [1]

[Turn to page 31 to see who wrote the quotes in this book.]

Money meant everything when you were in gaol. Prisons such as the Wood Street Counter had first-class and second-class cells, and a dungeon called 'The Hole' for the least fortunate prisoners. If you had money, you could invite friends to dine. One prisoner was even allowed to visit France, to buy cheap wine for his gaolers.

▲ These prisoners were held in Newgate for their religious beliefs. They could afford a comfortable cell, with some furniture.

London had fourteen prisons, including Newgate and Ludgate which were built into the city gates. By 1600 most towns had small gaols, though some were just a room in an inn. Some criminals chose to pay a groat (four pence) for a night's bed in a prison. It was the safest place to be if someone on the outside was chasing them.

◄ Newgate prison. Criminals called it 'Whittington' because it had been rebuilt with money from the will of London's famous mayor, Dick Whittington.

LONDON

The gaoler drags Hal from his cell, and boots him into the street. He shouts: 'Your money's bought you free – next time you'll hang!' Newgate's great door clangs shut, as Hal lands in the filthy, bustling London street. He begs a drink from a passing water-carrier, to wash the dust of gaol from his mouth.

Gaolers were often ex-criminals themselves. They ran their prisons like businesses, and sometimes the job passed from father to son. Gaolers brewed beer and baked bread to sell. Some of them ran gambling games. They charged prisoners for everything: unlocking the gates, taking irons off, even for water and light. However, if a debtor escaped, the chief gaoler or 'keeper' was often made to pay the runaway prisoner's debts.

Poverty was a major problem in Hal's time. The 'enclosure' of fields by rich landowners had reduced the land available to the poor. Many people travelled to London, where they begged and stole to survive.

◄ A Tudor gaoler. One gaoler was sent to Newgate for cruelty, and was placed in irons himself.

► A beggar and a rich landowner.

▲ South of the river, at Bermondsey in 1570, London still looked like a country village. Can you see the Tower of London in the distance?

To the north of the River Thames, London was growing into a large city. Housing was crowded, so people erected huts outside the city walls. The growing population led to an increase in crime. Among the criminals were soldiers and sailors who had been discharged from the forces.

'There is no country in the world where there are so many thieves and robbers as in England; insomuch that few venture to go alone in the country, excepting in the middle of the day, and fewer still in the towns at night, and least of all in London.' 2

London was not a healthy place to live. Foul-smelling pits served as toilets. Drinking water had to be bought from wandering water-carriers, who collected it from fountains such as the Conduit in Cheapside. In 1400, the Lord Mayor of London had 'caused sweet water to be conveyed to the gates of Newgate and Ludgate, for relief of the prisoners there'. But the prisoners, of course, had to pay for it.

▲ Led by his guide-dog, a blind water-carrier sells water from a long barrel.

LAW AND ORDER

Rounding a corner, Hal walks straight into the fat belly of Master Bradwell – the parish constable who recently arrested him. 'Only twelve summers old,' he mutters, 'and already like your poxy father.' He clips Hal's ear and walks on his way, his staff in hand and his keys jangling.

▲ Constables held dangerous criminals in irons: manacles for the hands, and shackles or fetters like these for the ankles.

To keep law and order, parishes elected a constable to serve for a year. He was given a short staff as a sign of office, and his duties included organizing the pursuit of criminals which was known as the 'hue and cry'. Constables were not paid, and few people wanted the job, but you could not refuse if you were elected. Many constables hired old men as deputies, to perform their duties for them.

◄ William Shakespeare's play *Much Ado About Nothing* (1599) features two comic constables, Dogberry (shown here) and Verges.

▶ The Court of Wards and Liveries, set up by Henry VIII in 1540, dealt with marriages and 'wards' (children with no parents). Can you spot the Tudor spectacles?

There were local courts in towns and villages where petty criminals like Hal were tried by Justices of the Peace (JPs). Tudor England had some 700 JPs, all untrained and unpaid. Four times a year, all the JPs of a county met in courts called Quarter Sessions. Here, convicted criminals were able to appeal against their sentences.

Royal judges visited each county twice a year for the 'Assizes', where serious crimes were tried in front of a jury. There were also 'Pie Powder' courts, which were held during markets and fairs. Here, cheating traders were punished. Brewers of bad ale, for example, had to drink their own beer or have it poured over their heads.

'John Sewell junr. of Great Dunmow ... did with violence and arms commit an assault upon a certain Robert Melford ... one of the constables of the same town ... because the said Robert by virtue of his office had then and there ordered the said John Sewell to desist from playing at a certain unlawful game called the football.' 3

▲ Judges travelled the country when they were not hearing cases in London. Once, in Oxford, two judges were among 300 people who died of 'gaol fever'.

10 am CONY-CATCHING

Hal strolls through St Paul's churchyard, which is crowded with booksellers. He is quickly greeted by a gentleman dressed in white holding out a box of cards. 'Care for a wager, my friend?' he leers. Hal recognizes the man as one of the many conmen or 'cony-catchers' who lurk here. These tricksters call their victims 'conies', which means rabbits.

In Tudor times, St Paul's Cathedral was a noisy, bustling building. Lawyers met their clients there. Traders used it as a short cut, through which to roll heavy barrels and lead their horses. Cony-catchers befriended country folk visiting the cathedral. They led them to taverns, then tricked their money from them.

◀ A well-dressed trickster wears parsley in his cap as a sign to other cony-catchers that he is looking for a 'rabbit'.

▶ A Tudor book showing cony-catchers picking locks, stealing purses, and cheating at cards.

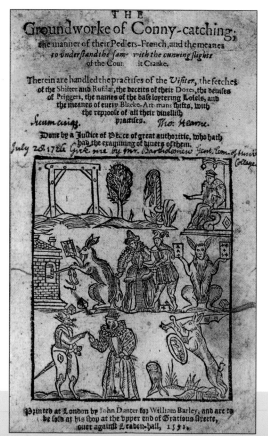

10

▲ A sermon is preached at St Paul's Cross. Whenever a crowd like this gathered, pickpockets carried out their trade.

'At divine service ... the nip and the foist, as devoutly as if he were some zealous person, standeth soberly, with his eyes elevated to Heaven, when his hand is either on the purse or in the pocket, surveying every corner of it for coin.' 4

The middle aisle of the cathedral, called Paul's Walk, was the criminals' meeting place. One Welshman, who had been tricked out of every penny by a gang, chased the thieves up and down the aisle with his dagger. Those cony-catchers who had not stolen enough to buy dinner stood by Duke Humphrey's tomb, looking miserable. This was known as 'dining with Duke Humphrey' – which meant eating nothing.

Paul's Church, as the cathedral was called, had a huge churchyard, the size of six football pitches. In the churchyard was Paul's Cross, where proclamations were read. Here, in 1588, it was announced that the English navy had defeated the Spanish Armada. A gallows was sometimes set up by the cathedral's west door, where murderers were hanged.

▼ Old St Paul's towered above the city. Before the spire was struck by lightning in 1561, you could climb to the top for a penny. One man named Banks even took his horse up.

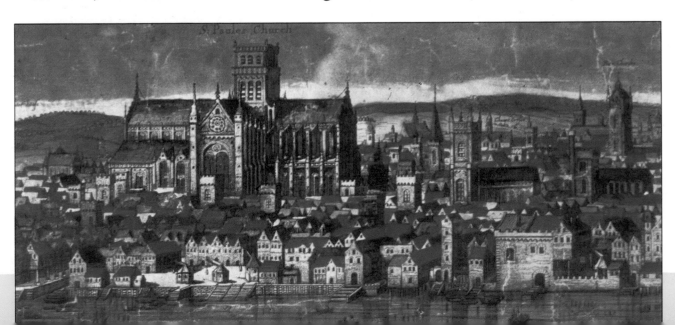

BEGGARS

A street seller calls: 'Hot mutton pies!' She turns her back for a moment, and Hal slips his dinner swiftly into his pocket. Hurrying away, he stumbles over a filthy beggar sitting in the street. The man is a 'palliard', and has smeared blood over himself from a pig's bladder. Now, he is rubbing his blistered arms with a yellow flower.

▲ Crowfoot was a herb used by beggars to make their skin look horrible.

'Hark, hark, the dogs do bark, the beggars are coming to town,' runs the old rhyme. Gangs of beggars roamed the countryside, stealing and terrorizing. The authorities called them 'vagabonds and rogues' and set up special prisons called 'Bridewells' where they were forced to work.

Beggars formed organized bands, which had their own sets of rules. New members were 'baptized' by having two pints of ale poured over their heads. Leaders called 'upright men' took a share of their followers' takings. The beggars even had their own language, which was called Pedlars' French.

◀ A 'palliard' or 'clapperdudgeon' was a beggar who used herbs and poisons to create sores on his body – so that people would give him more money.

PEDLARS' FRENCH

Beggars used the following words and phrases:

belly-cheat	apron
crashing cheats	teeth
doxies	female beggars
nip a bung	cut a purse
padder	highway robber
peck	food
prigger of prancers	horse thief
stamps	legs

▲ Nicholas Jennings in two of his disguises. When he was caught he was made to stand in the pillory first as an upright man, then as a counterfeit crank.

Beggars called 'counterfeit cranks' pretended to have 'falling sickness' or epilepsy. Some ate soap to make their mouths froth. One of the most famous was Nicholas Jennings, who begged enough to buy a house. Licences were given to beggars who were genuinely poor. Almshouses were set up where they could find food and shelter.

▲ Alms-boxes like this one were used to collect money or 'alms' for the poor.

'They take crowfoot, spearwort and salt, and, bruising these together, they lay them upon the place of the body which they desire to make sore. The skin by this means being fretted, they first clap a linen cloth, till it stick fast, which plucked off, the raw flesh hath ratsbane thrown upon it, to make it look ugly.' [5]

12 pm NIPPERS AND FOISTS

Hal climbs the outside staircase of a riverside alehouse. All eyes turn as he enters. A rogue with a pointed beard is surrounded by ragged children. Hanging from the ceiling is a purse, with bells on it. 'Show us your skill, Hal,' the rogue whispers. 'Show us what a real pickpocket can do!'

► Nippers used a dagger to cut purses from rich victims' belts. The smaller dagger is called a stiletto.

A school for pickpockets and cutpurses was set up in an alehouse near Billingsgate, by a gentleman rogue called Mr Wotton. His apprentices were trained to lift coins from a hanging pocket or purse without making the bells upon it ring. When they could do this, they were called 'foists' (pickpockets) or 'nippers' (cutpurses). Members of the thieving 'trade' held weekly meetings and paid insurance money. This bought their release from gaol if ever they were caught.

◄ A young foist practises lifting coins from a pocket, watched by a master thief.

▲ Rich ladies loved to display their wealth in fine jewellery, such as valuable chains. These were part of the 'Cheapside Hoard', found in the old goldsmiths' quarter of London.

'Of these two scurvy trades, the foist holdeth himself of the highest degree, and therefore they term themselves gentlemen foists, and so much disdain to be called cutpurses ... that the foist refuseth even to wear a knife about him to cut his meat withal.' [6]

A purse hanging from a belt was an easy target – it could be cut free or slit open. One cheeky cutpurse ordered a special knife, then cut the purse of the man who made it. A valuable chain was not so easy to steal. Another thief, after capturing a chain worth £57, said his 'teeth had watered' at seeing such a rich prize!

Mary Frith, known as 'Moll Cutpurse', was the most famous female thief. She was featured in two plays, and even performed in the theatres herself. In Newgate, she came close to being hanged, and it was said that she paid a £2,000 bribe to win her release.

◀ The infamous thief Moll Cutpurse often dressed as a man and smoked a pipe.

1 pm DANGEROUS STREETS

Hal arrives at the quayside of the Thames, where the watermen are ferrying passengers in their boats. Hal sees the 'cony-catcher' who spoke to him at St Paul's leading one poor fool into a tavern. Ignoring the cries of the beggar, Hal watches his friends practising their cutpurse skills.

The quayside is busy with people returning from market. Traders load their purchases from horse-drawn carts into small boats. The quayside is a dangerous place to be if you have a few coins to your name. How many different crimes can you spot taking place? (They are listed on page 31.)

THEATRES

As a trumpet sounds, Hal pays a penny and jostles inside the Globe theatre. The yard is crowded, and fine dandies sit on the stage itself. The players are performing *Henry V*. A bearded actor steps on to the stage, and challenges the heckling crowd. But Hal's eyes are elsewhere. 'You thievin' little foist!' yells a furious merchant. Hal bolts for the door.

▲ The playwright Thomas Nashe, who was imprisoned for criticizing the authorities in his plays.

Theatres like the Globe were hated by the authorities. They thought crowded playhouses encouraged crime, riots and plague. They also disliked actors, because they roamed the countryside like beggars. Officials spoke of actors as 'rogues and vagabonds'. Several playwrights of the time ended up in gaol, many of them for brawling. Even Shakespeare, as a young man, was charged with poaching. His revenge was to invent a foolish old JP called Justice Shallow, who appears in several of his plays.

◀ Pistol, a boasting soldier, is one of Shakespeare's comic characters in *Henry V*.

The Globe

The Bear Gardne

Southwark, south of the Thames, was called a 'liberty' because it was outside the control of the City of London. For this reason, theatres such as the Rose and the Globe were built there. There were five prisons in Southwark, including The Clink which was named after the noise made by fetters. 'Clink' is a nickname for prison that is still used today.

▲ A Tudor map of Southwark, showing the Bear Garden and the Globe. A new Globe has been built on this site, which you can visit.

▼ A bull and bear being baited by dogs.

At the Bear Garden, audiences enjoyed bloodthirsty entertainments. Bears fought with packs of dogs in the sport of bear-baiting. The bears' teeth were often 'broken short' to reduce injuries to the dogs. Fierce bears such as Harry Hunks and Tom of Lincoln became famous. Bull-baiting was also popular, and in the Tower of London even lions were baited.

'Then a number of great English mastiffs were brought in and shown first to the bear, which they afterwards baited one after another ... although they were much struck and mauled by the bear, they did not give in, but had to be pulled off by sheer force, and their muzzles forced open with long sticks.' 7

ROYALTY

Hal is almost knocked over as a carriage rumbles past. 'Out of the way!' hisses a sinister official in a large white ruff. Through the carriage window, Hal glimpses the white-powdered face, ginger wig, jewels and blackened teeth – it is 'Good Queen Bess' as the people call Queen Elizabeth.

Hal would have known little about serious crimes such as the plots against the life of Queen Elizabeth. King Philip of Spain was behind many of them, and his spies used a secret 'watergate' from the river to enter the Spanish ambassador's house. Elizabeth had her own secret service, headed by Sir Francis Walsingham. He had spies throughout London, and experts who deciphered the codes of traitors' letters.

▲ Sir Francis Walsingham was Elizabeth's 'spy master', who protected her from Spanish plots.

◄ Queen Elizabeth being carried in a procession. She loved meeting her people, and went on 'progresses' round the country.

The Tower of London was built during the reign of William the Conqueror. In Tudor times it held important prisoners. They usually arrived by river through Traitor's Gate. Many never left again, but were executed on Tower Hill or Tower Green. Underneath the White Tower was the torture chamber. Its terrible instruments included the rack, which was called the 'Duke of Exeter's daughter', after a previous Constable of the Tower.

▲ The Tower of London. Even Queen Elizabeth I, as a princess, was imprisoned here.

Royal blood did not keep you safe from Tudor justice. Two of Henry VIII's wives, Anne Boleyn and Catherine Howard, were executed at the Tower. In 1553, Lady Jane Grey, who ruled England for just nine days, was also beheaded there. From her cell, she could hear the noise of her own scaffold being built.

'Then the hangman kneeled down, and asked her forgiveness, whom she forgave most willingly. Then he willed her to stand upon the straw: which doing, she saw the block, then she said, "I pray you dispatch me quickly".' [8]

▶ Royal and noble prisoners had the 'privilege' of being beheaded. This block and axe were used for the task. At least it was quick.

5 *pm* PUNISHMENTS

▲ Some people had to wear this 'fool's mask' when they were placed in the stocks.

A jeering crowd surrounds the stocks, hurling stale bread and rotten vegetables at a cheating baker. 'Have your mouldy loaves back!' shrieks an angry, sharp-faced woman. Hal picks up the best loaves to save for his supper, but one is so hard that he cannot resist flinging it at the helpless baker.

Punishments were severe for quite small offences. Petty criminals were displayed for up to three days locked in the stocks (by their feet), in the pillory (by their head and arms), or even in a cage. Sometimes a card displayed their crime, for those people who could read. One set of stocks in Stafford was 10 metres long. Whipping-posts were also common, and London had at least sixty.

◀ Rotten loaves and vegetables are thrown at a baker who sold his customers mouldy bread. The stocks were a popular entertainment for passers-by.

◀ Anyone caught begging without a licence was whipped through the streets. If they failed to learn their lesson they faced hanging, as this picture reminds us.

Other punishments were ear-cropping, nose-slitting and branding with a hot iron. One unfortunate criminal in Exeter lost both ears, had his nostrils slit and the letter 'F' for felon branded on his face. Even 14-year-old children, if convicted of begging, could be whipped and burnt through the ear with a hot iron over two centimetres thick.

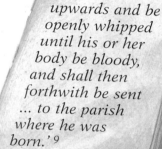

'Every rogue, vagabond or sturdy beggar which shall be taken wandering in any part of this realm shall be stripped naked from the middle upwards and be openly whipped until his or her body be bloody, and shall then forthwith be sent ... to the parish where he was born.' 9

Some nagging wives were forced to sit on a ducking-stool, a wooden see-saw which plunged the seat into a pond or river. Others were fitted with a 'scold's bridle', a metal head-piece which trapped their tongue.

▶ This musician is being treated well for entertaining the crowd. He may be in the stocks for using his music to distract people while a partner picked their pockets.

EXECUTIONS

The gallows is thankfully a long way from where Hal is standing. 'Can't you look, boy?' an innkeeper laughs. But Hal remembers the prisoner's scared face in Newgate that morning. The executioner, Mr Bull, does his work as the delighted crowd roars. Another victim hangs from Tyburn Tree, and Hal rubs his neck thoughtfully.

▲ A man hangs from the gallows. Three gallows were often built in a triangle. The nickname for the gallows was 'three trees and a ladder'.

It was possible to be hanged for stealing goods worth just a shilling. One woman was hanged for stealing two sheets. It was said that 'many lose their lives for scarce as much coins as will hide their palm'. In one year there could be as many as 800 hangings.

A terrible punishment for crimes against the country, or treason, was to be 'hanged, drawn and quartered'. The traitor was hanged by the neck, then cut down while still alive and 'drawn' or disembowelled. The body was finally cut into four quarters. The head was displayed on a pole, as a grisly warning to others.

◀ A hangman prepares his rope. Public hangmen, such as London's Mr Bull, became famous.

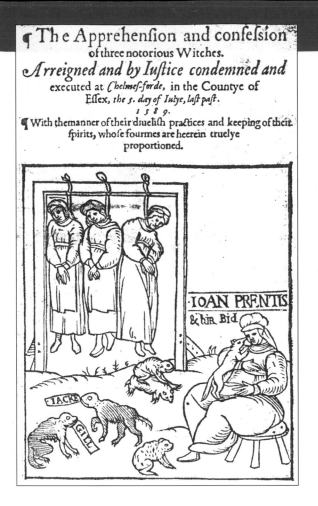

◀ A book cover showing three witches being hanged at Chelmsford, in Essex. Their animals or 'familiars' are also shown.

People accused of witchcraft also faced the gallows. Many were just lonely old women with pets. The Tudors were superstitious and believed animals like cats or frogs could help a witch cast her spells. One form of trial was called 'swimming a witch'. The accused was thrown into a river. If she sank, she was pronounced innocent – but she was likely to drown!

There were many terrible forms of execution. 'Bloody' Mary Tudor, who reigned from 1553 to 1558, had 300 people burnt at the stake for their religious beliefs. Women who had poisoned their husbands were burnt alive. Other poisoners were boiled to death in water or lead.

'Upon Friday last we sat at the Justice Hall at Newgate from seven in the morning until seven at night, where were condemned certain horse-stealers, cutpurses and suchlike to the number of ten, whereof nine were executed.' 10

◀ The gory heads of traitors were displayed on poles, usually over this gateway on London Bridge. One foreign visitor in 1598 counted thirty of these heads.

ALEHOUSES

Hal's father calls over the 'pot-boy' to pour out more ale. The Bear and Ragged Staff alehouse is full of smoke from people's pipes – the latest fashion. Hal's father is a well-known thief. He watches the games of cards and dice, and points out the cheating tricks to Hal.

▲ The Feathers Inn, at Ludlow, has changed little since Tudor times.

Respectable inns, and the not so respectable alehouses, were very much part of daily life – especially for criminals. People drank enormous quantities of beer, ale and wine. Servants in large houses were allowed a gallon (4.5 litres) of beer daily. Women and youngsters preferred ale, which was not so bitter.

Roads between towns were badly kept, and it was dangerous to travel alone. Innkeepers, and the 'ostlers' who looked after guests' horses, were often working in league with local robbers. They checked to see which travellers were worth robbing, then tipped off the highwaymen. In return, they received a share of the robbers' takings.

◀ A young servant pouring wine into a glass, which was a rare luxury. Beer was often served in leather mugs called 'blackjacks'.

Carmine fit uiuax uirtus, experfq; fepuicbri.
    Notitiam feræ pofteritatis babet:
Tabida confumit ferrum lapidemq; uetuftas,
    Nullaq; res maius tempore robur habet.
Scripta ferunt annos, feriptis Agamenona noftit
    Et quifquis contra, uel fimul arma tulit.
Quis Thebas, feptfq; duces fine carmine noffet?
    Et quicquid poft hæc, quicquid et antè fuit?
Dij quoq; carminibus, fi fas eft dicere, fiunt:
    Tantaq; maieftas ore canentis eget.

Pon. 4

'I believe not that [any] traveller in England is robbed by the way without the knowledge of some innkeeper ... For when the traveller comes into the inn, the ostler is very busy to take down his baggage – whereby he gets an inkling whether it be money. Then he gives warning to such odd guests as haunt the house.' 11

◀ A Tudor playing card, showing the 'muse' or goddess of love poetry.

Gambling was common in alehouses, and so was cheating. Cards were pinched, bent, pricked, or marked with ink-spots. Cheats spied on other players' hands. They used a mirror on the wall, or accomplices made secret signs – one woman moved her sewing needle in a special way. False dice were also used. They were weighted with lead or spiked with bristles to make them land on certain numbers. Such dice were made in the Marshalsea and King's Bench prisons!

▼ The stakes in this card game between gentlemen and ladies were probably quite high.

THE WATCH

As night falls, Hal keeps to the shadows. He sees a well-dressed rogue scamper by clutching a purse, followed by the old, wheezing watchman waving a pistol. Hal sneaks into Whitefriars, where all pickpockets are welcome. A straw pallet is better than Newgate's cold stones. The watchman cries: 'Ten o'clock, look well to your locks.'

▼ Some rich people defended their homes with a pistol like this one.

After dark, the streets were even more dangerous than usual. Footpads lurked, waiting to ambush passers-by. Reaching home was no guarantee of safety. Thieves called 'hookers' used hooks on the ends of long poles to lift clothes and valuables out through the open windows of houses.

At night, travellers could hire a 'link boy' with a lighted torch to guide them home, although it was the duty of every householder to put a light in front of their property. The rich were also expected to keep weapons such as pistols which could be used to apprehend criminals.

◄ John Selman, a famous cutpurse, is shown here with the pickings of his trade. He is dressed fashionably, and does not look like a criminal.

◀ A watchman's lamp. The top end of the pole was filled with burning oil, or with wood covered in pitch.

'A hooker came to a farmer's house in the dead of the night, and putting back a draw window of a low chamber ... in which lay three persons ... this hooker with his staff plucked off their garments which lay upon them to keep them warm, with the coverlet and the sheet, and left them lying asleep naked saving their shirts.' [12]

At nightfall, as Bow Bells chimed, the city gates were shut. The day constables or 'ward' were replaced by the night watchmen or 'watch'. They collected their brown bills and lanthorns from Ludgate. A curfew was enforced which meant that everyone had to be indoors, and late travellers were challenged. Anyone arrested was taken to the constable early the next morning. But many of the old watchmen were too lazy to arrest anyone.

There were certain areas of the city where watchmen would not venture. These criminal quarters or 'liberties' included Southwark, Whitefriars, Newington Butts (where archery was practised) and the brick-kilns near Islington. Criminals within these areas had a well-organized intelligence system, and used the Pedlars' French language of the beggars.

▶ A watchman with his lanthorn, brown bill and bell. Watchmen or 'bellmen' patrolled the streets throughout the night, calling the hours.

GLOSSARY

almshouses	Houses built for poor people, usually paid for with donations from the rich.
beadle	A parish officer with various jobs, including policing.
brown bill	A watchman's pole with a curved blade and spikes.
Cheapside	A wide London street with a large market and some fine buildings.
coverlet	The top covering of a bed or piece of furniture.
cutpurse	A thief, particularly one who cuts purses from people's belts.
felon	A violent criminal.
footpad	A criminal who attacks his victims on foot, often knocking them unconscious.
gaol	The old spelling of jail.
gaol fever	A form of typhoid which often spread rapidly in prisons.
lanthorn	The Tudor word for lantern – light shone through thin pieces of horn instead of glass.
mastiffs	Large, strong dogs, used for fighting.
pallet	A straw bed, or mattress.
pot-boy	A young servant in an inn, who brought the customers' drinks.
poxy	A slang term for worthless. The 'pox' was a disease.
ratsbane	Rat poison, or arsenic.
ruff	A starched frill worn round the neck.
Tyburn Tree	The usual place for hangings in London.
watermen	The 2,000 ferrymen who provided a river 'taxi service' in Tudor London.

Use a dictionary to find out more about the origins and meanings of some words used in this book: thumbscrew, flogged (p. 4); Armada (p. 11); vagabonds (p. 12); alms, pillory (p. 13); foist (p. 14); ambassador, progress (p. 20); curfew (p. 29).

BOOKS TO READ

Look inside a Shakespearean Theatre by Peter Chrisp (Wayland, 1998)
Stories of Tudor Times by Alan Childs (Anglia Young Books, 1995)
The Poor in Tudor England by Jane Shuter (Heinemann, 1995)
Tudor London by Rosemary Weinstein (Museum of London: HMSO, 1994)

Children can use this book to improve their literacy skills in the following ways:

 To compare the fictional opening paragraphs with the non-fiction text, noting differences in style and structure (Year 3, Term 1, non-fiction reading comprehension).

 To understand that vocabulary changes over time, by looking at Tudor words and criminal slang which are little used today (Year 4, Term 2, vocabulary extension).

 To use the footnoted quotes as an example of how authors record their sources (Year 5, Term 2, non-fiction reading comprehension).

 To explore the use of biography through the role of the historical character Hal (Year 6, Term 1, non-fiction reading comprehension and writing composition).

TIMELINE

1485   The first Tudor monarch, Henry VII, comes to the throne.

1509   Henry VIII becomes king.

1536   Henry VIII passes a law to brand beggars.

1540   The Court of Wards and Liveries is set up.

1549   Labourers in Norfolk rebel against common land being enclosed.

1552   Gilbert Walker publishes the book *A Manifest Detection of Dice Play*.

1553   The first Bridewell is set up.

1561   St Paul's church spire is struck by lightning and collapses.

1563   A law is passed against witchcraft.

1570   Moll Cutpurse is born, the daughter of a shoemaker.

1572   An act is passed to punish vagabonds, including actors or 'players'.

1577   Two judges die of gaol fever in Oxford.

1582   A report is made on Mr Wotton's school for pickpockets.

1585   John Sewell goes to court for assaulting a constable who stopped him playing football.

1589   Angry soldiers attack London, and the trained bands are called out to restore order.

1591   Robert Green publishes the book *The Second Part of Cony-Catching*.

1593   JPs investigate 'excessive prices' charged by gaolers.

1597   The Act for the Punishment of Rogues, Vagabonds and Sturdy Beggars says that beggars should be whipped or banished to galley ships.

1601   The Poor Law Act. Parishes collect taxes to pay for relief for the sick and aged, and to provide work for the able-bodied.

1603   The death of Queen Elizabeth I ends the Tudor age.

CRIMES

The crimes shown on pages 16–17 are (left to right) a cutpurse lifting a purse; a hooker stealing a pot through a window; a palliard with false wounds begging; a cony-catcher conning somebody; and a footpad beating and robbing his victim.

SOURCES OF QUOTES

1. William Fennor, *The Counter's Commonwealth* (1617).
2. An Italian visiting England at the beginning of the Tudor period (Camden Society, 1847).
3. Essex Record Office: *Indictment at Quarter Sessions* (1585).
4. Robert Green, *The Second Part of Cony-catching* (1591).
5. Thomas Dekker, *O per se O* (1612).
6. Robert Green, *The Second Part of Cony-catching* (1591).
7. *Thomas Platter's Travels in England*, 1599, ed. Clare Williams (Cape, 1937).
8. An account of Lady Jane Grey's execution, from *The Chronicle of Two Years of Queen Mary*, 1554, quoted in the *Harleian mss 194*.
9. *An Act for the Punishment of Rogues, Vagabonds and Sturdy Beggars* (1597).
10. Recorder Fleetwood to Lord Burghley (1582).
11. William Harrison, *A Description of England in Holinshed's Chronicles* (1577-87), ed. F.J. Furnival (1877).
12. Thomas Harman, *A Caveat for Common Cursitors* (1566).

INDEX